W9-DHY-096

FITCH & CHIP

Who's Afraid of Granny Wolf?

Book #3

Story by Lisa Wheeler

Pictures by Frank Ansley

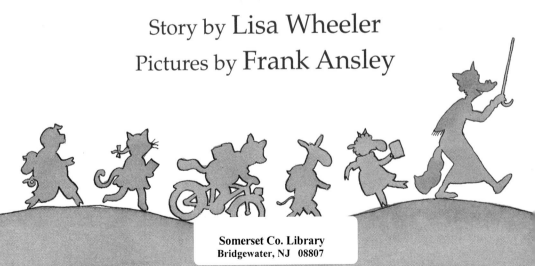

A Richard Jackson Book
Atheneum Books for Young Readers
New York London Toronto Sydney

Atheneum Books for Young Readers
An imprint of Simon & Schuster Children's Publishing Division
1230 Avenue of the Americas
New York, New York 10020
Book design by Abelardo Martínez
The text of this book is set in Palatino.
The illustrations are rendered in ink and watercolor.
Manufactured in the United States of America
First Edition
2 4 6 8 10 9 7 5 3 1
Library of Congress Cataloging-in-Publication Data
Wheeler, Lisa, 1963–
Who's afraid of Granny Wolf? / Lisa Wheeler ; illustrated by Frank Ansley.—1st ed.
p.   cm. — (Fitch & chip ; 3)
"A Richard Jackson Book."
Summary: Eager to see all the differences between a wolf's house and a pig's, Chip has
dinner with Fitch and his grandmother and, after a few misunderstandings, discovers
how much they have in common.
ISBN 0-689-84952-4
[1. Wolves—Fiction. 2. Pigs—Fiction. 3. Dwellings—Fiction. 4. Grandmothers—Fiction.]
I. Title: Who is afraid of Granny Wolf?. II. Ansley, Frank, ill. III. Title.
PZ7.W565Wj 2004
[E]—dc21
2003013011

In loving memory of my grandma, Mary Budai (1916–2001), who didn't bother with fake teeth
—L. W.

For Avery
—F. A.

Contents

1.

Wee! Wee! Wee!

Chip skipped down the sidewalk.

"Wee! Wee! Wee!" he sang.

"I am going to Fitch's house! Weeeeeee!"

Fitch skipped too.

He hurried to keep up with Chip.

"It is just a regular house," said Fitch.

"It is a wolf's house!" Chip said.

"And I will meet your granny."

"She is just a regular granny," said Fitch.

"She is a wolf granny!" said Chip.

"I wonder what she looks like."

"Like a granny," Fitch said.

"Like a *wolf* granny!" said Chip.

"I wonder what we will eat for dinner?"

"Food," said Fitch.

"We will eat food."

"Wolf food?" asked Chip.

"Regular food," said Fitch.

"Will your granny eat, too?" asked Chip.

"Of course," said Fitch.

"I wonder what a granny wolf
  likes to eat," said Chip.

"I wonder, I wonder . . ."

Chip stopped skipping.

He walked slowly.

He was very quiet.

Fitch stopped skipping, too.

He was very unquiet.

"Do not worry. We will have

fun," said Fitch. "Lots and

lots of fun!"

He patted Chip's shoulder.

"My granny will love you!"

"Baked or boiled?" asked Chip.

Fitch laughed.

"You are such a funny pig!" he said.

"Here we are! Come on in."

2.

Something Different

"I have been in three kinds of houses,"

Chip said.

"Straw, wood, and brick.

But I have never been in a wolf house."

Fitch showed Chip around.

"Here is the kitchen," said Fitch.

Chip looked at Fitch's kitchen.

"You have a regular sink

and a regular stove," said Chip.

"Just like my house."

"Everybody has a sink and stove,"

said Fitch.

"I thought a wolf's kitchen

would be different," said Chip.

Fitch looked around

for something different.

He pointed to the refrigerator.

"Granny has twelve

frying-pan magnets.

That big one is from Howlywood."

"*Wow!*" said Chip. "Howlywood!"

Fitch smiled proudly.

"We *tape* notes to our refrigerator," said Chip.

"Magnets are different."

Fitch showed Chip the bathroom.

"You have a regular tub
and a regular toilet," said Chip.

"All bathrooms do," Fitch said.

Chip sighed.

"I thought a wolf's bathroom

would be different."

"We have this," Fitch said.

He opened the door a bit wider.

Behind the door stood a rack

full of magazines.

"Cool!" said Chip.

"We do not have magazines

in our bathroom.

Wolf bathrooms are the best!"

Fitch showed Chip the den.

"Your den is regular, too," said Chip.

"Regular chairs,

regular lamps,

a regular couch . . ."

That is when Chip

saw something different.

He saw a regular granny wolf

sleeping on the regular couch!

3.

Granny Wolf

"Shhh," said Fitch. "Granny is napping."

"Can I watch?" asked Chip.

"Why?" asked Fitch.

"I never saw a granny wolf before,"
  said Chip.

"It is something different."

"We must be quiet," whispered Fitch.

"*Zzzz-wooo-aghhh.*" Granny Wolf snored.

Her nose wrinkled with each Zzzz.

"What a long nose she has,"

whispered Chip.

"Just like the Lobo side of the family,"

Fitch said.

"They all have long noses."

"*Zzzz-wooo-aghhh.*" Granny Wolf snored.

Her ears wiggled with each *Wooo*.

"What long ears she has!" said Chip.

"She is old," whispered Fitch.

"Granny says her body is shrinking,

but her ears keep growing."

"*Zzzz-wooo-aghhh.*" Granny Wolf snored.

Her teeth showed with each *Aghhh.*

"What looong, white teeth she has!"

Chip forgot to whisper.

"Shhh," warned Fitch. "They are fake."

"Fake teeth!?" Chip cried.

"Who ever heard of a wolf

with fake teeth?"

"False teeth," Granny Wolf said.

"They are called *false* teeth."

Granny Wolf was awake!

4.

Something Pig

Granny Wolf sat up on the couch.

"You must be Chip," she said.

Chip watched Granny's *false* teeth.

They wiggled around in her mouth.

"I am pleased to eat you,"

she said with her wiggly teeth.

"Eat me?" cried Chip.

"No, no, no!" said Granny Wolf.

She pushed up on her wiggly teeth.

"Meet you! I am pleased to meet you."

"Oh," said Chip.

"I am p-p-pleased to meet you, too."

"We did not mean to wake you,"

said Fitch.

"That is okay. It is near dinnertime,"

said Granny.

Her false teeth wiggled about.

"I am cooking some thin pig!"

"Pig!" said Chip.

"You are cooking some thin pig?"

"No, no, no," said Granny Wolf.

"Excuse these silly teeth."

She pressed them again.

"I am cooking *something* BIG.

B-I-G."

"Oh," said Chip.

His cheeks were now apple red.

"I am not v-v-very hungry."

"Too bad," said Granny.

"My kettle has been over the fire all day."

"Will we have dessert?"

asked Fitch.

"Yes," said Granny Wolf.

Her false teeth wiggled to and fro.

"Chunk of Chip pie."

"No!" cried Chip.

"I do not want to be a pie!"

Chip ran toward the door.

His cheeks were both as red as beets.

"*Chocolate*-chip pie!" cried Granny Wolf,

pressing on her false teeth.

"I made chocolate-chip pie!"

Chip stopped at the door.

"Chocolate-chip pie?" he said.

"Yes," said Granny Wolf.

Chip looked at Fitch.

"I have never had chocolate-chip pie,"

he said.

"It is something different."

"Granny's pie is the best," Fitch said.

He patted Chip's shoulder.

"I will stay," Chip said.

"Good," said Granny Wolf.

"And I will go fix these silly teeth."

5.

Just the Same

Fitch, Chip, and Granny Wolf

sat at the table.

Fitch sipped soup from a spoon.

Chip sipped soup from a spoon.

Granny sipped soup from a spoon.

"This is very good soup," said Chip.

"Thank you," said Granny.

"It is my regular vegetable soup."

Granny dipped her bread into her soup.

Chip dipped his bread into his soup.

"This is a very good house," said Chip.

"Thank you," said Granny.

"It is just a regular house."

"Oh, no," Chip said.

"You have a magazine rack.

Your bathroom is just like

a doctor's office!"

"A doctor's office?" said Granny.

"I have never thought of it that way."

Granny took a bite of her bread.

Chip took a bite of his bread.

"You have a magnet from Howlywood,"
said Chip.

"Your kitchen is like an art museum!"

"I have never been to a museum,"
Granny said.

"I have never been to Howlywood,"
said Chip.

They both sipped a spoonful of soup.

"I like visiting new places," said Granny.

"Me too," said Chip. "I like

new places."

"Then you are just

the same!" Fitch said.

"I guess we are!"

Granny smiled at Chip.

Chip crumbled bread into his soup.

"I can take you to the art museum."

Granny crumbled bread into her soup.

"That would be nice," she said.

"Can I come, too?" asked Fitch.

"Of course!" said Chip.

"It will be something different

for both of you."

"But we will like it just the same,"

said Granny Wolf.

"Just the same!" said Fitch and Chip.

Then they all had a piece

of Granny's chocolate-chip pie—

just the same size:

B-I-G!

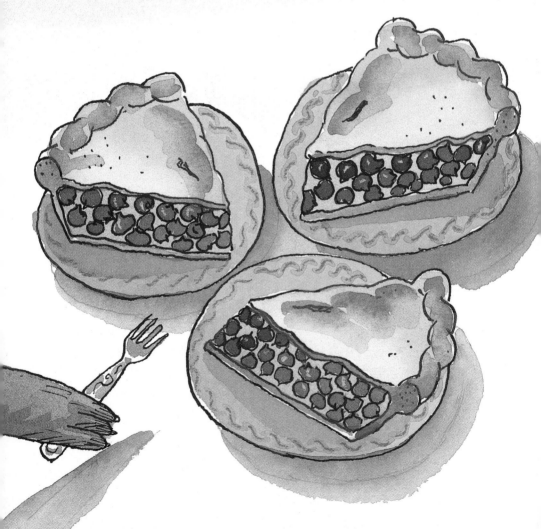